I0518711

The Toy Maker

Inkwolf Press

J. A. Campbell

Published by Inkwolf Press
P.O. Box 251
Severance, Colorado
80546-0251

www.inkwolfpress.com
www.writerjacampbell.com

PRODUCED IN THE UNITED STATES OF AMERICA

10 9 8 7 6 5 4 3 2 1

Dedication

For Bobby, who's heart is as big as the Toy Maker's.

Acknowledgements

I wanted to thank David B. Riley for setting up the Steampunk Christmas event that prompted me to write this story. Also, thank you to the fine folks at the Broadway Book Mall in Denver for hosting the event and all of your support.

Vivian Trask and Sam Knight, thank you for your edits. As always, your red pens make my stories so much better. Devin O'Branagan, thank you also for your edits and your help with formatting.

A very special thank you to Shoshanah Holl. The cover and interior art...just...wow...Your work is amazing. Thank you.

As always, thank you reader. Without you, these stories would be hidden away on my hard drive or tucked into a corner in my mind.

The Toy Maker

"We aren't going to leave today." Nicholas despaired. He held open the drapes and stared out of the window into the swirling snow. He had come to the city market to sell his toys for the holiday like he did every winter. The toys provided for him and his wife for the year. Nicholas wiped a tear from his eye. Next year he would have only himself to provide for. Martha's health had faded quickly and he had hoped only to be gone a couple of weeks. Now it looked like he might not get home before Christmas.

Sighing, he let the drape swing shut and went back to his table by the fireplace in the common room. Picking up a piece of wood, he returned to his carving of a horse. Trapped by the storm, there wasn't much else to do. He didn't have any materials to craft his mechanical toys and everything that needed repairing in the inn he'd fixed days ago.

"Oh, honey." Matilda the innkeeper came out of the back room bringing him a steaming mug of cider. "The storm will clear this afternoon. You'll be on your way before you know it. It's a good thing that wagon of yours has runners though, or you'd be stuck here until spring."

Nicholas grinned at the rosy woman. "I'd ride poor old Rudy if it came to that."

"I'm certain you would." She patted him on the shoulder. "Gunter and Greta will love the toys. They are so clever. Greta adores horses and Gunter always dreams of dragons."

Nicholas had traded two of his mechanical toys, running on gears and levers and a bit of steam, to the innkeepers in exchange for his room and board for the duration of the storm. Otherwise the cost would have drained his earnings, and he enjoyed making the children happy. He wished he could see their expressions when they received their gifts on Christmas, but he was anxious to get home and couldn't spare the time.

Holding up the partially carved horse, Nicholas said, "I will leave this with you, if I finish it in time. I don't believe I've created anything so simple in years, but I'm enjoying the exercise."

"That's very kind of you, Nicholas. It will grace the mantel over the fireplace." She patted him on the shoulder again and went to wipe nonexistent dirt away from the tables and counters that made up the cozy inn.

Nicholas carved another slice away from the piece of wood, revealing the horse, sliver by sliver.

"What did I say?" Matilda grinned at Nicholas. "You even have time to make it to Steinhalt if you hurry."

Weak sunlight, a welcome change from the blinding white snow, shone as Nicholas completed his carving. "I intend to. Thank you so much for your hospitality," he replied. "For you." He held out the carved horse. "If I come through again, I will paint it."

Matilda's smile lit her face and warmed Nicholas's heart.

"I'd better get Rudy steamed up and hitched." Nicholas shrugged his old cloak over his shoulders and pulled on his thick gloves.

"There's plenty of split wood in the shed, please take some. You've more than repaid us for your stay."

Normally, Nicholas would not have accepted, but it would save him time and he needed to return quickly to his wife. "Thank you."

The chilly air nipped at his exposed cheeks as he left the inn, but the sunshine warmed him. He smiled as he stomped through the snow to the barn where his wagon and Rudy waited.

Nicholas patted the horse's metal shoulder. "Rudy, my friend, let's get you steaming."

Rudy's eye swiveled and an ear twitched, but he did not have enough power for anything else, yet.

Nicholas flipped up the hatch on the big horse's boiler and loaded in as much wood as would fit. Next he secured the hatch and pushed the igniter. After a moment, steam hissed and Rudy's nose glowed red.

The mechanical horse neighed and pawed the ground as the steam built, anxious to be on his way.

"Easy there, we'll be on the trail soon enough."

Nicholas checked the harness and found it secure. Finally he loaded enough wood into the wagon to get him home.

"Okay, Rudy, take her out." Nicholas stepped back to give Rudy room.

The mechanical complied with a toss of his head, pulling the wagon out into the snow.

Nicholas shut the barn door and climbed into his sleigh. He pulled the lever that raised the wheels above the level of the runners, and the wagon, now a sleigh, settled into the snow. He took up the reins and flicked them, urging Rudy forward a few more steps.

"Nicholas!" Matilda waved from the doorway. "Here,

before you leave."

Rudy pulled the sleigh to the front of the inn and stopped, issuing a steamy nicker as Matilda came out into the snow with a basket in her hands.

"Provisions for a few days."

"Matilda, you've already given me fuel for my journey."

"Yes, fuel for your wonderful Rudy, now here is fuel for you. Take care, and we look forward to seeing you next year."

Matilda placed the basket in his sleigh and stepped back, the cool air turning her cheeks pink. She waved.

Nicholas pushed one more button and the magnets that held the small balls inside the sleigh bells released. The merry jingle filled the town as he and Rudy trotted toward home.

Nicholas silenced the bells as the sleigh passed the edge of town and slowed when he noticed a stooped figure plodding through the snow, dark cloak standing out against the white landscape. He pulled his sleigh alongside and stopped.

"It's a cold day to be walking anywhere," he called down. "Would you like a ride?"

The hood slipped back a little revealing a wizened old lady. "I'm going to the next town to see my daughter and her new baby for the holidays. Walking was my only option." Her voice crackled with age but her eyes shone bright.

"Please, I'm going that way myself. Let me take you. This snow is too deep to walk in for very long."

"Thank you, kind sir."

He helped the old woman up into the sleigh, and tucked the blanket around her legs.

"I'm Nicholas."

"Agathe. I can't thank you enough, Nicholas. Why did you silence your sleigh bells?"

He laughed. "You don't always want to announce your presence so loudly when you're traveling long distances in the forest."

"Ahh, very wise, young man."

They passed the rest of the trip in pleasant conversation, pausing only to add more wood to Rudy's boiler, and before too long they reached the edge of Steinhalt. He pushed the button to release the bells and jingles filled the air.

Children ran to windows and a few came outside as they trotted through the middle of town. People waved and a few called greetings.

"You are known here?" Agathe asked.

"Yes, I passed through on my way to the city market. I sold a few of my toys."

The old lady considered him for a few moments. Nicholas forced himself to hold her penetrating gaze as much as he could and still direct Rudy.

"My daughter's place is on the edge of town just as you're about to leave. Won't you stay with us for the night? I know she won't mind."

"No, but thank you for the offer. I must press on. My wife is poorly and I wish to get home. I believe there are some farms I can seek shelter at before the light fades completely."

Nicholas pulled up to the small cottage, and briefly considered changing his mind. Smoke from the chimney promised relief from the deep chill, but no, he had to keep going.

"Please, take this as a thank you for giving an old lady a ride." She held out a plain wooden bowl.

Nicholas's hand tingled when she handed the bowl to him.

"When you are hungry, you have only to think of food and the bowl will fill with stew or porridge."

"I couldn't possibly accept such a treasure."

"No, keep it. I have another." Agathe laughed and walked away before he could object.

Nicholas climbed back into his sleigh, and, after making sure the old woman got inside, he slapped the reins across Rudy's metal back.

"Home, old friend."

Steam snorted from Rudy's nostrils as the mechanical horse headed toward their distant home.

"I wonder how a woman who couldn't afford to hire a ride came to have two magical bowls."

The mechanical horse didn't answer.

The red glow from Rudy's nose illuminated their path once darkness fell. Although Nicholas wanted to press on, the cold seeped into his bones and forced him to start looking for a place to spend the night. Finally he saw a break in the trees and smelled wood smoke. A small cottage sat off the main road a short distance. He directed Rudy down the path and halted in front of the door. Setting the brake, he climbed down, boots sinking almost to the tops in the snow.

He knocked, and presently the door opened a crack.

"Hello?" A frail voice inquired.

"Hello, I'm Nicholas. I was hoping for a place to stay for the evening. May I sleep on the floor by your fire?"

"Young man, its freezing out there, come in. We don't have much to offer but of course you may sleep by our fire." The old woman opened the door farther.

Nicholas didn't correct the woman, compared to her he was a young man, but he felt most of his fifty years every day. "Let me grab a couple of things from my sleigh and shut it down for the night and I will be right in."

Quickly, Nicholas cared for Rudy, bringing his boiler to a low steam so he'd be ready to go quickly in the morning and he threw a cover over the sleigh and his mechanical horse, who whickered with a last bit of steam. Then he grabbed the basket of provisions.

The old couple introduced themselves as Mr. and Mrs. Kistner. They'd lived in the area for most of their lives and at one time Mr. Kistner had been a woodcutter. Now they made do as best they could, but winter was hard on them, and they had very little food in the house.

Nicholas was happy to share his provisions, keeping only enough to see him home and they passed the evening in happy conversation, telling Nicholas of younger times and all the travelers who had sheltered with them on this road.

Nicholas slept well with his back facing the banked fire and the next morning he was up early, bringing Rudy's boiler up to full steam so they could get an early start. He packed the tarp away in the sleigh and came across the wooden bowl Agathe had given him. He had enough food to see him home, and he'd made enough money on his toy sales to get them through the year. This old couple needed a steady food supply more than he did.

Taking it back inside, he presented it to Mr. Kistner. "I want you to have this."

Mr. Kistner accepted the bowl, squinting at it. "It's a fine bowl, thank you."

Nicholas smiled. "I haven't tried it myself, but the old woman who gave it to me said you had only to think of stew or porridge and it would be full."

Before Mr. Kistner could say anything, the bowl magically filled with porridge. His eyes went wide and Mrs. Kistner gasped.

"Son, we couldn't possibly accept such a gift." Mr. Kistner tried to hand it back, but Nicholas put his hands behind his back.

"You have more need of it than I do. Please. It would make me happy to know that you will always have food."

Mrs. Kistner glanced at her husband. They both nodded as if having a private conversation. Then Mrs. Kistner went to one of her cupboards and pulled out a plain wooden cup, blowing off a little dust.

"We will accept your gift, if you will accept ours."

Curious, Nicholas took the cup.

"This cup will cure the drinker of all ailments."

He tried to hand it back. "I couldn't possibly…"

"No, take it son, we've both used it once and it only works three times. With only one use left, it isn't any good to us. What good is healing one of us, when the other will receive no cure? No, we've had a good long life, take it and use it for a great need."

"Thank you." Nicholas's hands shook as he held the cup. More anxious than ever to return home, he clutched his wife's cure to his chest.

"Now, be on your way. You have to get home to that young lady of yours." The old couple shooed him out the door and waved as Rudy pulled the sleigh away.

The forest closed in around him, and the gray sky was gloomy, but lightness filled Nicholas's heart. He would be home the next day and what a gift he had for his wife.

Nicholas and Rudy made good time and their long day of travel was uneventful. Darkness fell early, though the days were finally starting to lengthen, and Nicholas was starting to think about finding a place to stay when Rudy's red nose illuminated a narrow path from the main road and Nicholas smelled the telltale scent of wood smoke.

Almost without his bidding, Rudy turned down the path and halted in front of the door of the little cottage.

Nicholas climbed down from his sleigh and knocked on the door.

A young man opened the door a crack.

"Hello, I was wondering if I could rest here for the night," Nicholas said. "I can pay."

The man glanced inside before opening the door.

"Nonsense. We're happy to have you. Come in."

"I'm Nicholas," he said once he was inside the warm cottage.

"This is Nadja my wife, and I am Oskar. My daughter, Rebekka is in the other room. She's very ill." Oskar's smile faded.

"What is wrong with her?" Nicholas asked, wondering if he should move on. He didn't want to expose his wife to any illnesses.

"A wasting disease. Nothing can be done," Nadja said quietly. "Would you like to meet her? She loves visitors."

"Of course." He decided to stay. A wasting disease wouldn't be contagious.

"Here, let me take your cloak and you can warm yourself by the fire," Oskar said.

"And I will go wake Rebekka." Nadja left the room.

"Let me get something out of my sleigh and cover it for the night." Nicholas left the house and pulled out the tarp, covering Rudy and his sleigh. Before he went back inside, he took one of his remaining unsold toys, a Pegasus that walked and had wings that flapped, and was about to turn away when he remembered the cup. The cup that would cure any illness, and only had one charge left. The cure for Matilda.

Heart heavy, he put the cup into his pocket. He knew what his wife would want.

Back inside, he handed over his cloak and held up the toy Pegasus for Oskar to see.

"May I give her this? I make toys for a living and this is one that hasn't sold yet."

"It's too much," Oskar said, but his eyes lit up with interest as he took the mechanical toy and inspected it. "How does it work?"

"A small bit of wood in the boiler there." He pointed at the port. "It's quite safe, doesn't overheat and won't over-steam. This button here makes it walk, and this works the wings."

"Fascinating."

"Please, I would like your daughter to have it."

"If you're certain, I know she'll love it. Come, this way." He handed the toy back and led Nicholas down a short hallway.

Nicholas followed Oskar to another room. The little bed sat close to a fireplace. A small figure lay huddled in tightly wrapped blankets close to the warmth.

"Rebekka, the toy maker has come to visit us, and he brought you something."

The girl was petite, fragile with skin so pale it was almost white as the snow. Dark circles made her eyes look shrunken and lank blonde hair framed her face.

"Hello, Toymaker." The little girl turned the title Oskar had given him into a name.

Her musical voice broke Nicholas's heart. That one so sick, should sound so joyful….

"Hello, Rebekka. Have you been a good girl this year?"

"I'm trying, but it's hard to get into trouble when you're sick anyway." She laughed, before a coughing fit took her. She gasped for a few minutes before her eyes focused on Nicholas again.

He gently sat on the bed next to her and held out the Pegasus toy.

Her eyes went wide. "For me?"

"Yes. You'll have to give her a name of course, and take good care of her. But she likes little girls the best. She told me so herself when I made her."

Tears welled in the little girl's eyes as she took the Pegasus toy and held it close, being careful of the wings.

"I will think of the best name ever. Thank you!"

Her eyes drooped and she yawned.

"I'll let you rest now, Rebekka."

"Thank you, Toymaker." Her voice, momentarily strengthened with her excitement, faded again. Her eyes flickered shut.

Nadja took the Pegasus and put it on the small table next to the bed.

Tears shone in both parents' eyes when they led Nicholas to the kitchen.

"It won't be long now, but I'm glad she got to meet you. Let's have some dinner before it gets too late."

The family had plenty of provisions, so Nicholas didn't feel bad eating their food, but he was quiet for most of the dinner, thinking about the cup and the little girl. Finally, he knew he had to give it to them. His wife would be horrified if he told her of the child and would no doubt make him turn around and bring the cup back instead of drinking from it herself. He could trick her, but he felt she'd never forgive him, and truly, what else could he do? This child had her whole life ahead of her, or she would once she drank from the cup.

"Oskar, Nadja, I was given something on my trip home that might help Rebekka." He held out the plain wooden cup. "An old couple told me that it would heal anyone of any illness, but that it only had one use left. I want you to have it for Rebekka."

They both stared at him. Oskar frowned and leaned back before glancing at his wife.

"Truly?" Nadja finally said.

"I know only what I was told. At this point, perhaps it

couldn't hurt to try?" Nicholas didn't mention that he had planned to give it to his wife. They didn't need to know.

Nadja grabbed the cup from his hand and rushed to the water basin.

"Forgive her," Oskar said, sounding embarrassed.

"Nothing to forgive," Nicholas said as Nadja hurried from the room.

She returned a few moments later, sitting back at the table and staring at her hands. "I suppose we will have to wait and see now. Even if it doesn't work…that you would share this with us…thank you." Her voice broke and Oskar put his arm around her and helped her from the room as she sobbed.

Nicholas hoped it did work. He retired to a spot in front of the fire. He was about to lay out his cloak to get a little rest when he heard someone clear their throat.

"Mr. Toymaker, could you show me how she works? She told me she wants to fly."

Nicholas turned and saw little Rebekka standing there holding out the Pegasus.

"Well, of course." He took the toy from her, studying the child as he did so. The dark circles had vanished from under her eyes, and though she was still thin, some color had returned to her cheeks. "Why don't you run and get your parents and I'll show you all."

Rebekka grinned and did as he said. Nicholas was willing to bet she hadn't run in quite some time.

"We can't thank you enough." Nadja clutched a grinning Rebekka to her, though the girl squirmed, ready to run and play.

"Just seeing her healthy again is thanks enough."

"Before you leave," Oskar said, coming out of the house with a red bundle in his arms. "I noticed your cloak is getting thin. I know this color is bright, but I want you to have this." He held out the red bundle.

Nicholas took it and saw the grandest fur-lined cloak he'd ever seen. The outside was a warm, thick, red material and the inside the whitest fur. He'd never be cold wearing it.

"I can't possibly…" He tried to hand it back.

"No, I am a tailor and I made this. A noble commissioned it, but after it was finished decided he didn't like red after all. No one in this area could possibly buy it. I want to give it to you. You've given us so much."

Seeing that the man would not be deterred, Nicholas removed his old cloak and settled the new one on his shoulders. Already he was much warmer, and he smiled and shook hands with Oskar and gave Rebekka a quick hug before she finally escaped and ran up to Rudy, patting him on his metal shoulder. The mechanical horse lowered his head and nudged the little girl, sending her into a giggling fit.

"I must be on my way; my wife awaits."

"We wish you all the best, Nicholas. Please, drop by anytime."

"I'll do that," Nicholas said and climbed into his sleigh. He pushed the button to release the bells, and Rudy trotted away to a merry jingle tune.

The hours dragged, but finally Nicholas neared his home. Again he let the jingle bells sound. Martha, would be listening for them, as she could no longer watch for him to come home. The sickness had long since taken her sight along with her vitality. She would join the angels soon, but he hoped he could see her one last time.

Pushing Rudy to the mechanical horse's top speed as he reached the turn to his own cottage in the forest, Nicholas held his breath, hoping Martha waited. Neighing out steam, the horse pranced and made the bells ring to their fullest.

His small cottage came into view and his heart filled with joy at the light burning in the window. Asking Rudy for one last burst of speed, they hurried down the path before coming to a halt right outside his front door.

"I will care for you in a moment, old friend," he said to the mechanical horse, before he opened his front door.

"Martha!"

"Oh, Nicholas, how wonderful. I heard the bells, and knew you had returned to me." Martha sat next to the fire bundled in a cushioned chair he had built for her years ago. Her eyes stared blankly ahead out of her gaunt face as they had for a few years, but she turned her face toward his voice and smiled.

Trying not to let his voice show his despair at how she had deteriorated in the weeks he'd been gone, he came and wrapped her in a hug. "Dearest, I'm so happy to see you."

"What's this? A new cloak?" she asked, touching the material.

"Yes, my journey home was quite a story. I'll tell it to you. Is there anything you need?"

"No, Nan took care of everything before she left for the day. Take me for a ride in the sleigh and tell me your story."

"Martha, you must rest."

She sighed. "Nicholas, I'd like one last ride. We both know this will be my last Christmas. What can it hurt?"

"Very well." Nicholas, fighting tears, picked up his wife, amazed at how little she weighed, and carried her out of the house. First he took her over to say hello to Rudy. The horse nudged his wife gently and she smiled as she rubbed his nose. Then he wrapped the new cloak around her and the old one around himself. She snuggled against him as he asked Rudy to circle the house. He didn't want to go far in case she needed to go back inside quickly.

"The storm delayed me and when I finally set out…" Nicholas related how he'd given the old woman a ride, and the bowl she'd gifted him. Then he talked about the old couple he'd given it to, and the healing cup. Her hand tightened on his arm when he mentioned it, but she said nothing, waiting, probably knowing that if he still had it, he would have given it to her right away. Tears squeezed from his eyes, and he wondered if he had done the right thing.

As soon as he mentioned the sick little girl her grip on his arm loosened.

"Of course, and you gave the cure to the little girl."

"Yes, dearest. I did."

She smiled, and his heart eased. "I knew I'd married you for a reason. How wonderful."

There was no hesitation in her voice, and Nicholas knew he'd done the right thing.

"And now I am home and we have enough money to

eat and buy supplies for the next season of toy making."

"Wonderful." Her smile was as beautiful as the day he'd met her. He wiped another tear from his eye.

Martha fell silent, and Nicholas asked Rudy for one more circuit of the house. He would take her inside and spend the rest of her days with her, but once she was gone, he didn't know how he could make another toy again. She was his inspiration, his passion, and without her, well, he just didn't think it would be the same.

Martha's breathing settled to the steady rhythm of sleep, and Nicholas guided the sleigh to his front door, intending to take his wife inside. Before he could get out, a bright light appeared before him, glowing so brightly he had to shield his eyes. The light hovered in the air, reflecting off the snow and making Rudy's metal back shine. Slowly the radiance diminished until he could look straight at it, and after he blinked tears from his eyes, he made out small figure silhouetted by the illumination.

"Have you come to take my wife?" Nicholas put his arms protectively around Martha, thinking the being was an angel.

"No, Nicholas," the creature said, its voice feminine and musical and vaguely familiar. "I'm here for you."

"But who will take care of Martha?"

"Silly." The creature laughed. "I'm not the death angel. Rather, I have an offer for you. You have proven that you are selfless, kindhearted and a talented toy maker who likes to make people happy. We have need of one such as you."

"How…how do you know?"

For a moment the glow behind the angel faded and he could make out her features. He saw the wizened old woman he had given a ride!

"Agathe?"

The glow returned, hiding her features again, and she laughed. "That is one of my names, yes. You have passed all of our tests, and we want you to join us."

"I won't leave my wife. Maybe…maybe after…" He couldn't finish the thought.

"Your lovely wife is welcome to join you."

"What is this offer?" Nicholas was curious.

"To make toys for all the children of the world."

Ignoring the impossibility of that task, Nicholas asked, "Where do we have to go?"

"Far north."

"I couldn't possibly."

"Have faith, Nicholas. If you accept, we will get you there."

"Very well, I accept. But not until my wife can travel." Accepting couldn't hurt. She'd never be well enough to travel and once she was gone, what reason did he have to stay?

The angel laughed again. "Easily accomplished. Do you need anything? You won't be returning."

Nicholas frowned. "Martha's keepsake chest is our only true treasure besides my tools."

"Gather your things, Nicholas. The night is wasting."

Hesitantly, he climbed from the sleigh, making sure Martha was still bundled in his cloak. He didn't believe any of this was happening. Once inside he stared around the house he'd built with Martha. The chairs he'd carved, the mantel they'd decorated with treasures from the forest and small carvings he'd made for her. How could he leave all this behind at the behest of an angel?

After a moment he decided he had nothing to lose. How could he live amongst his memories once his wife was gone? It was worth a chance that the angel could heal his wife, and if not he could return. Nicholas gathered Martha's chest and his tools and brought them back to the sleigh. When he climbed in, the angel sprinkled glittery powder over Rudy, and then the sleigh. Rudy reared, jostling the sleigh before settling. The mechanical turned his head this way and that and swiveled his ears as if listening to someone speak that only he could hear.

"Rudy knows where to go, Nicholas. Let his red nose lead the way, and by the time you land, your wife will be well." The angel vanished in a brief flare of light.

Not knowing what else to do, Nicholas slapped the reins gently across Rudy's back. The mechanical horse neighed, blowing steam from his nose. He trotted a few steps before pulling the sleigh into the air.

Nicholas gasped.

Martha woke and looked around, eyes wide with wonder.

"What a beautiful night, Nicholas." Her voice sounded strong, like it had before the sickness took her.

Tears blurred his eyes, and he laughed as Rudy guided his sleigh through the sky, toward the far north. With Martha healthy at his side, he was certain he could accomplish anything, including making toys for all the children of the world.

Delivering them—well, that was a problem for another day.

About The Author

Julie has been many things over the last few years, from college student, to bookstore clerk and an over the road trucker. She's worked as a 911 dispatcher and in computer tech support, but through it all she's been a writer and when she's not out riding horses, she can usually be found sitting in front of her computer. She lives in Colorado with her three cats, her vampire-hunting dog, Kira, her Traveler in Training, Triska, and her Irish Sailor. She is the author of many Vampire and Ghost-Hunting Dog stories and the young adult urban fantasy series The Clanless as well as the Tales of the Travelers young adult fantasy series. She's a member of the Horror Writers Association and the Dog Writers of America Association and the editor for Steampunk Trails fiction magazine. You can find out more about her at her website: www.writerjacampbell.com.

Other Books

Tales of the Travelers
- Sabaska's Tale
- Sabaska's Quest

Legends of the Travelers
- Saga

Doc Vampire Hunting Dog
- The Moths of Miller Place
- Camping Tales

Into the West

Brown, Ghost Hunting Dog Collection

Sky Yarns
- Serpent Queen

Clanless Series
- Senior Year Bites
- Summer Break Blues
- Freshman Year Freaks

Various Short Stories

Darkness Taken - Dragonthology

The Baron and the Firebird – Happily Ever Afterlife

The Martian Menace of 1897 – Science Fiction Trails 11

The Life – Six Guns Straight From Hell
(Written as Dakota Brown)

Doc Vampire Hunting Dog, Sheep Interrupted –These Vampires Don't Sparkle II

The Toy Maker

The Perfect Pastry

Tales of the Travelers

Sabaska's Tale

J. A. Campbell

Untold Press

To Anna, horses were more than a fascination, they were everything. Luckily, she had the opportunity to spend every summer on her grandmother's horse ranch in Colorado. Life was perfect, until she received the devastating news that her grandmother had been tragically killed. Anna knew she was the only member of her family who could take over the ranch and hopefully find new homes for her grandmother's beloved Arabians. Anna wasn't alone for long. Her grandmother had hired a local teenage boy to help tend the horses for the summer. Anna didn't stand a chance against Cody's quiet charm and the two rapidly become friends. however, even with the responsibilities of the ranch, Anna quickly discovers the secrets her grandmother had been hiding and a legacy that sends her on an adventure she never thought possible. An adventure in the saddle of a horse that wasn't a horse at all. Sabaska, her grandmother's favorite Arabian, was a Traveler; a magical being that could travel between worlds. With Anna at the reins, they find themselves trapped in a fight against evil with the highest of stakes… Their very survival.

Have a ghost problem? Brown is the dog for the job. Normally used to herd sheep, her Border Collie Eye works on ghosts, too. Follow her adventures as she and her human, Elliott, hunt ghosts all over the old west. They find their first real ghost in a saloon in Miller, Colorado, and from there her nose leads her to more adventures.

Brown fights ghosts on trains, boats, and in old mines. She discovers that some ghosts are friendly when she and Elliott need extra help fighting a magical construct. There may be friendly ghosts, but there are no friendly Martians, and Brown has to take the ultimate adventure to save Elliott from their nefarious clutches, meeting new friends along the way.

Packed full of adventure, this weird western anthology contains seven short stories and one never before published novella.

Taken from her people as a foal, Saga is plunged into a world completely foreign to her. All Travelers know other worlds exist, but they don't expect to actually experience them until they are adults. Saga must learn to adapt to her new surroundings if she wants to survive until she's old enough to be able to Travel among worlds and return to her people.

Jarl is the son of the Vanir High Mages and heir to the throne. Though young, his parents entrust him with the care and training of the captured Traveler foal. However, none of the Vanir understand just how intelligent the Travelers are and they may have given Jarl more than he can handle.

When Saga escapes, the High Mages decide she is too much trouble and has to be killed. Jarl defies his parents and goes after her. Will they remain enemies when Jarl finds her, or will they form a bond of friendship strong enough to save Saga's life?

www.ingramcontent.com/pod-product-compliance
Lightning Source LLC
Chambersburg PA
CBHW070654130626
46555CB00006B/2867